Lily Gets Lost!

Jane Simmons

ORCHARD

Spring was in the air
and everything was buzzing.
When Lily heard a nibbling
behind the hedge she thought,
"Who could nibble such a nibble?"

Lily had to see.

She pushed through the hedge
and there, on the other side, was a rabbit,
ears twitching and nose wiggling.

Lily twitched and wiggled, too.

Hippity, hop, hopped the rabbit.
Lily hopped too,
around the orchard with all the rabbits.

hippity, hoppity, hippity, hop!

When Lily heard a snort
behind the bushes she thought,
"Who could snort such a snort?"
Lilly just had to see.

"Mooo! Mooo! Mooo!" mooed the cows.
Lily mooed too, "Mooo!"

Mooo!

Lily heard a splash behind the reeds.
Who could splosh such a splash?
Lily had to see.

"Quack! Quack! Quack!" quacked the ducks.
Lily quacked too, "Quack!"
But all the ducklings raced back to their mamma,

and suddenly Lily missed her mamma too.
Where was Mamma?
Lily had to see . . .

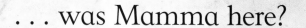

. . . was Mamma here?

No, there were only donkeys in the paddock.

"Eey-or, EEY-OR!" they bellowed so loudly it frightened her.

"MAAAA?" Lily cried and ran away
as fast as she could.

Eey-or!

EEY-OR!

Was Mamma here?
"MAA MAAAA!" Lily called,
but a deep rumble came from the shadows.

Grrrrunt!

Lily gasped!
Who could grunt such a grunt?

MAAAAAA!

Lily didn't want to see!
"MAAAAAA! MAAA!" Lily wailed.

"Grunt, oink, grunt," went the piglets.
"Shush now!" grunted Mamma Pig kindly and
the piglets shushed. And Lily shushed.
The barn fell silent and noises from outside
floated in, an eey-or, a splash and a snort.

"Listen carefully now," said Mamma Pig.
Lily listened carefully past the quack, past the moo
and far, far away she heard a "Baa! Baa! Baaa!"
Who could Baa such a Baa?

"Mammaa!" she cried and ran out of the barn,

past the
Eey-orr!

past the
QUACK!

. . . all the way back to Mamma.
"Lily!" said Mamma. "Where have you been?"
And Lily thought, 'Oink, Eey-or, quack, moooo!'
but all she could say was . . .